Disney's
CHIP 'N' DALE
RESCUE RANGERS

FAKE ME TO YOUR LEADER

D0923296

Twin Books

B. Mitchell

Adapted by
Naomi McMillan

Illustrated by
Vaccaro Associates, Inc.

Cover illustration by
Jim Mitchell

Designed by
Gary Albright

At Ranger headquarters, Gadget put the finishing touches on the new Ranger Rocket. "Zipper," she asked, "are you sure you're strong enough to handle the launching gear by yourself?"

Zipper felt insulted. He grabbed the slingshot launcher and began to pull as hard as he could.

Meanwhile, Chip, Dale, and Monterey Jack raced to the launchpad to see the test flight. "Hurry!" said Dale. We're gonna miss it!"

But it was too late. Zipper and the rocket came crashing down even as Dale spoke.

"You should've waited for us!" Chip scolded Zipper.
"Yeah!" griped Dale. "You're too puny for this kind of job!"
Zipper hung his head in embarrassment, looking down at
the broken bits of machinery all around them.

The next morning, Zipper decided it was time for him to get in shape. He ran on a treadmill, jumped rope, and even tried lifting a barbell. Monterey Jack was watching. "Well, look at that," mumbled the big mouse, feeling sorry for his friend. "Me little pal is trying to build up his body!"

But it was just no use. Zipper would never be as strong as the other Rangers, and he knew it. He was just too small.

Zipper sadly flew off to the nearby junkyard to be by himself. Lost in thought, he sat on an old car that was being towed away. When it jerked to a stop, Zipper was thrown to the ground. There he found himself face-to-face with several pill bugs—and the shoes of Norton Nimnul, the evil scientist.

"Why, what ugly little bugs!" said Nimnul. "I can't wait to zap them with my gigantico ray gun and make them ugly *big* bugs!"

Zipper knew he had to get out of there fast. But no sooner had he begun flapping his wings than he and the pill bugs were bathed in a strange bright light. Nimnul scooped the dazed pill bugs into a jar while Zipper managed to escape, unseen.

When Zipper got back to headquarters, there was a surprise waiting for him.

"I whipped up one of me specialties—to build up your muscles,"
Monterey Jack told him. "Melon rind à la Monterey. This'll put some
meat on your bones!"

Zipper dived into the melon and picked it clean.
"I think he looks bigger already," noted Chip.
"You know," said Gadget slowly, "he *does* look different."

The next day, the Rescue Rangers struggled to lift the repaired rocket back onto the launchpad.

"Heave!" yelled Gadget.

"Ho!" grunted the others.

16

Then Zipper appeared, lifted the plane easily, and flew up into the trees.

The Rescue Rangers were stunned. Zipper was ten times his normal size.

Meanwhile, the pill bugs, now six feet tall, were chomping on every piece of wood in Nimnul's workshop. The scientist aimed his ray gun at the bugs and shrank them back to normal size. "Can't you see I have work to do?" he said angrily.

18

Next, he busied himself attaching a cylinder of helium to an inner tube. Then he tied the inner tube to a bus. In no time he had inflated the tube, which lifted the bus right off the ground. "It works!" he shouted. "It works!"

Back at Ranger headquarters, Chip was watching a news bulletin on television.

"Today," said a reporter, "a spaceship landed on City Hall. Its captain demanded ten tons of gold from the mayor."

"Bring us the gold or we will invade the Earth!" threatened the creature. Its voice came through a speaker at the front of the spaceship, which looked amazingly like a floating bus.

"I'm sure I've heard that alien's voice somewhere before,"
said Chip. "We'd better get down to City Hall and take a closer
look!" Chip led the gang out to the rocket launch site.

"Let's get on board!" said Gadget. Without thinking, Zipper jumped on top of the rocket and crushed it beneath him. "Now how are we going to get to City Hall?" moaned Chip. Zipper had the perfect solution.

The Rangers flew into the city on Zipper's back. Dale thought
it was a great way to fly until a woman below pointed up at Zipper
and screamed. In no time, police sirens filled the air.
"We'd better get out of here!" yelled Chip.

But as Zipper zoomed around a corner, the Rescue Rangers slid off his back and into a trash can. Zipper panicked and flew into a nearby clothing store to hide.

"Send in the SWAT team!" yelled the chief of police.

The SWAT team lined up in front of the clothing store while Zipper
huddled inside. He was shaking with fear.

"You have one minute to give yourself up," shouted the police chief,
"or we're coming in!"

The other Rescue Rangers scrambled out of the trash can and rushed into the revolving door of the store. The SWAT team pushed in right behind them, and the Rangers found themselves on the sidewalk once again.

The SWAT team searched the store. The sergeant saw a figure
in a coat, hat, and sunglasses. It was Zipper!

The sergeant asked him if he had seen any aliens, but Zipper
just shook his head. Then the sergeant warned him to be careful.
Zipper nodded and slipped out the door.

Outside, Chip said, "Poor Zipper! What'll we do?"
"He'll just have to go away until he shrinks back," said Dale.
They didn't know that Zipper had heard every word.

That night, the Rangers went back to City Hall to investigate the spaceship.

"Wait a minute! This flying saucer is made out of rubber!" said Chip, bouncing on the inner tube.

"Wow! Look at this!" said Monterey, swinging the door open. Inside, the bars of gold had already been delivered.

Nimnul came running. "What's going on here?" he shouted.

"Hey, that's the same voice as the alien's!" Chip said.

Nimnul grabbed the Rangers and locked them in the glove compartment of the bus. But Monterey had an idea. He stuck his tail in the lock and jiggled it until the door dropped open.

The Rangers ran straight for the microphone that hooked up to the loudspeaker, shouting all at once. "It's a trick! The aliens are fake! It's all a hoax!" But no one heard them.

Nimnul chased the Rangers with a rolled-up newspaper,
but when he swung, they grabbed the paper and crawled inside.
"Now where'd they go?" asked Nimnul.
He tossed the newspaper over his shoulder, and the Rescue
Rangers hit the ground with a thud.

When they crawled out, they saw two gigantic bugs coming right at them. Then Nimnul pointed his gigantico ray gun at the insects, and it bathed them in a circle of light. Instantly, the bugs shrank back to normal size.

"I think I know what made Zipper get so big," said Chip.

All at once, the "spaceship" lurched. Zipper, now fifty feet tall, had landed on top of the bus and was peering in the window.

As he launched the ship, Nimnul ripped the inner tube on the tower of a tall building. Helium began to escape from the inner tube. Then gold bars began to spill out of the bus.

Nimnul parachuted away. The rolled-up newspaper holding
the Rangers went into a nose dive..

"Quick!" said Gadget. "Help me fold this thing!" Soon the four landed safely in their homemade paper airplane.

In the meantime, Zipper was in the middle of the inner tube, his wings pinned flat. But he landed unharmed, and within moments the scientist and his parachute landed right in his hand. With police sirens closing in behind him, Zipper tore down the street. He saw a nearby skyscraper and climbed to the top, Nimnul squirming in his grasp.

Meanwhile, Chip, Dale, Gadget, and Monterey had landed right beside Nimnul's gigantico ray gun. "We can use this to get Zipper back to normal," said Chip. They grabbed the gun and raced to the skyscraper.

"We've got to get to the top floor!" yelled Chip, leading the
way to the elevator.

Monterey pushed a potted plant next to the control panel,
and Dale climbed up the stalk and hit the button.

The Rangers ran out onto the observation deck.
"Zipper, look out!" Chip screamed. The tower Zipper was on crumpled, and he and Nimnul began to fall.

Gadget set the gun on reverse, and aimed it at Zipper. *Zap!*
Zipper shrank back to his normal size, and dropped through the
inner tube. He flapped his wings and slowly rose into the air.

Below, Nimnul grabbed the inner tube and tried desperately
to inflate it with a bicycle pump.

Moments later, a reporter stood in front of the skyscraper. "The aliens and their spaceship have vanished, leaving the gold behind! Was this entire incident just a joke?" he asked. "We may never know."

Nimnul, meanwhile, crept away and stole a car parked nearby.
"They may have foiled my plan," said Nimnul as he sped off, "but
they'll never foil *me!* "

Zipper flew up to meet his friends on the observation deck.
"We weren't a team without you, Zipper!" said Gadget.
"Right!" agreed Dale. "We can always use somebody exactly your size!"
Zipper just smiled.